I dedicate this book to our children of today
and of future generations—J.S.

For friends and family, who helped
make this book possible—E.P.

Text copyright © 1995 by Chief Jake Swamp
Illustrations copyright © 1995 by Erwin Printup, Jr.
All rights reserved. No part of the contents of this book may be reproduced
by any means without the written permission of the publisher.
LEE & LOW BOOKS, Inc., 95 Madison Avenue, New York, NY 10016

Printed in the United States of America on recycled paper

Book Design by Christy Hale
Book Production by Our House

The text is set in Globe Gothic Demi
The illustrations are rendered in acrylic on canvas

10 9 8 7 6 5 4 3 2
First Edition

Library of Congress Cataloging-in-Publication Data
Swamp, Chief Jake,
Giving thanks: A Native American good morning message/by Chief Jake Swamp;
illustrated by Erwin Printup, Jr.—1st ed.
p. cm.
ISBN 1-880000-15-6 (hardcover)
1. Mohawk Indians—Juvenile literature. 2. Human ecology—Juvenile literature.
3. Nature—Religious aspects—Juvenile literature.
I. Printup, Erwin. II. Title.
E99.M8S83 1995
299'.74—dc20   94-5955
CIP AC

AUTHOR'S NOTE

The words in this book are based on the Thanksgiving Address, an ancient message of peace and appreciation of Mother Earth and all her inhabitants. These words of thanks come to us from the Native people known as the *Haudenosaunee,* also known as the *Iroquois* or Six Nations—Mohawk, Oneida, Cayuga, Onondaga, Seneca, and Tuscarora. The people of the Six Nations are from upstate New York and Canada. These words are still spoken at ceremonial and governmental gatherings held by the Six Nations.

Children, too, are taught to greet the world each morning by saying thank you to all living things. They learn that according to Native American tradition, people everywhere are embraced as family. Our diversity, like all the wonders of Nature, is truly a gift for which we are thankful.

To be a human being is an honor, and
we offer thanksgiving for all the gifts of life.

Mother Earth, we thank you for giving us everything we need.

Thank you, deep blue waters around Mother Earth,
for you are the force that takes thirst away from
all living things.

We give thanks to green grasses that feel so good against our bare feet, for the cool beauty you bring to Mother Earth's floor.

Thank you, good foods from Mother Earth,
our life sustainers, for making us happy
when we are hungry.

Fruits and berries, we thank you for your color and sweetness. We are all thankful to good medicine herbs, for healing us when we are sick.

Thank you, all the animals in the world,
for keeping our precious forests clean.
All the trees in the world, we are thankful for

the shade and warmth you give us.
Thank you, all the birds in the world, for singing
your beautiful songs for all to enjoy.

We give thanks to you, gentle Four Winds,

for bringing clean air for us to breathe
from the four directions.

Thank you, Grandfather Thunder Beings,

Thank you, Grandmother Moon,
for growing full every month

your light and warming Mother Earth.

Elder Brother Sun, we send thanks for shining

for bringing rains to help all living things grow.

to light the darkness for children
and sparkling waters.

We give you thanks, twinkling stars,
for making the night sky so beautiful

and for sprinkling morning dew drops
on the plants.

Spirit Protectors of our past and present,
we thank you for showing us ways to live in
peace and harmony with one another.

And most of all, thank you, Great Spirit, for
giving us all these wonderful gifts, so we will be
happy and healthy every day and every night.